PUFFIN BOOKS

THE GREAT PIRATICAL RUMBUSTIFICATION
AND
THE LIBR...
AND THE R...

In the first of these two amazing narratives, spring is in the air, and all the pirates in town are getting restless longing for one of their special parties, or *rumbustifications*, as they like to call them. Then Mr and Mrs Terrapin phone the agency for a baby-sitter, and unknowingly set the scene for the greatest rumbustification ever. For their sitter has half the usual number of legs, a patch over one eye and a bottle of rum in his pocket!

In the second story, a lovely librarian deals with her vile kidnappers by the only means at her disposal: the deadly disease of Raging Measles and a love of fine literature.

Margaret Mahy's wildly improbable and wonderfully witty stories are just the thing for everyone who likes a good laugh. And, of course, Quentin Blake's illustrations are the very ones to bring all these amazing events to life.

Margaret Mahy is a New Zealander who has been writing stories from the age of seven. She has twice won the Carnegie Medal. She has two grown-up daughters, several cats and thousands of books. She lives near Christchurch, South Island, in a house she partly built herself.

Other books by Margaret Mahy

MARGARET MAHY

THE GREAT PIRATICAL RUMBUSTIFICATION

& THE LIBRARIAN AND THE ROBBERS

WITH PICTURES BY QUENTIN BLAKE

PUFFIN BOOKS

PUFFIN BOOKS

Published by the Penguin Group
Penguin Books Ltd, 27 Wrights Lane, London W8 5TZ, England
Penguin Books USA Inc., 375 Hudson Street, New York, New York 10014, USA
Penguin Books Australia Ltd, Ringwood, Victoria, Australia
Penguin Books Canada Ltd, 10 Alcorn Avenue, Toronto, Ontario, Canada M4V 3B2
Penguin Books (NZ) Ltd, 182–190 Wairau Road, Auckland 10, New Zealand

Penguin Books Ltd, Registered Offices: Harmondsworth, Middlesex, England

First published by J. M. Dent & Sons Limited 1978
Published in Puffin Books 1981
20 19 18 17 16 15 14 13 12 11

Printed in England by Clays Ltd, St Ives plc
Set in Monotype Baskerville

THE
GREAT
PIRATICAL
RUMBUSTIFICATION

*

A STORY
IN THIRTEEN LUCKY
CHAPTERS

1. The Pirates are Restless

All over the town the pirates were getting restless. 'Yo, ho, ho!' they whispered in the lifts, the lofts and the lordly streets of the city.

These weren't the impulsive young pirates, mind you, but the older pirates who had retired from the sea to live on their ill-gotten riches.

That is why they were restless; it was months since there had been a pirate party.

The pirates were longing for Pirate Rum and for steaming bowls of Pirate Stew – a wonderful stew where every pirate puts something good into the pot ... a turnip, a bunch of carrots, mushrooms or a bottle of wine.

It is a great piratical delicacy.

The sign of a pirate party is a message in the sky – the words 'Pirate Party', written over the stars.

Every night now the pirates studied the sky, but nothing was written there.

'O for a pirate party!' the pirates grumbled ominously, trying their swords for sharpness.

All the pirates – Roving Tom, Wild Jack Clegg, Rumbling Dick Rover, Orpheus Clinker and Old, Old, Oldest-of-all, Terrible Crabmeat – were restless with longing for a great Rumbustification.

The whole city was churning with restless pirates. The difficulty was that a pirate party must be a STOLEN one.

2. The Terrapins are Restless Too

Perhaps it was spring, slowly softening the city with pink blossom and little, young leaves.

Perhaps the pirates were spreading restlessness everywhere like measles.

In one particular house in the city there was a particular lot of more restlessness: it was the Terrapin House.

Mr Terrapin was restless because it was a new house, a new big house, a new, big, old house.

It was old in years. It was big in rooms. It was new because the Terrapin family had just moved into it. It was new in the way of being different from the small flat they used to live in.

It had cost Mr Terrapin more than he cared to think about.

When he did think about it, by accident, he turned green and went all limp.

'I must have been mad!' he would whisper to himself. 'I was talked into it.'

The people who had talked him into it were his wife, Mrs Terrapin, and his sons Alpha, Oliver and Omega.

'I'll never pay it off, never!' he would whisper, growing greener and limper at the thought. When he wasn't green he was restless.

His sons, Alpha, Oliver and Omega, were restless too, but for a different reason. When they had lived in the flat and tried to do anything adventurous their mother would say:

'*Do* wait my dears, until we have a bigger house. Then you can expand.' (No adventures were allowed in flats, only in big houses.)

Now they had had a bigger house for more than three weeks. Alpha, Oliver and Omega had waited, but nothing had happened, just the ordinary things like bed, school and washing.

A man needs more than washing in his life.

Alpha, Oliver and Omega did their best to make things lively – but they needed cooperation. Their mother tried, but her heart wasn't in it. Their father tried, but if you mentioned money he went green and limp and had to sit down.

The boys couldn't help feeling restless, too.

The pirates, the Terrapins – everywhere

restlessness and discontent, spoiling the city springtime.

Then, at last, things began to happen.

3. *Mr Terrapin Comes Home Early*

Mr Terrapin came home early. He was in a hurry, but he could tell at once that this had been a busy and interesting day for his dear sons.

Someone had painted a pink elephant on his green front door.

Someone had put glue on the doormat.

Someone had covered the door handle with jam.

'Oh, well,' said Mr Terrapin licking his fingers, 'Boys will be boys ... ah, raspberry – the jam I like best.'

Mr Terrapin climbed nimbly in at the window.

'Darling,' he called to Mrs Terrapin, 'Darling – Millicent! Put on your fur coat, my love, and paint your face. We're going out.'

Mrs Millicent Terrapin was tied to the leg of the table with dressing-gown cords. Alpha, Oliver and little Omega danced around the room wearing warpaint and pyjama trousers.

'Had a good day, dear?' asked Mr Terrapin. 'Now, boys, untie your mother. I want to take her out.'

'You've come just in time, Daddy,' said Alpha. 'Now we're going to set fire to the table.'

'There's no time for that at the moment,' said Mr Terrapin, smiling fondly at his three adventure-loving sons. 'How soon can you be ready, Millie?'

'Well, really, my dear,' said Mrs Terrapin as Oliver ungagged her, 'I don't know if I can. No, no – I can't leave my children just to gratify a wish for a bit of idle pleasure.'

'Get a baby-sitter, Millie,' commanded Mr Terrapin, looking at his watch. 'This is an important dinner. A rich man – Sir John himself – is going to be there. I want to watch him closely and see if I can guess how he made his riches.

Ring the Mother Goose Baby-Sitting Service, if the phone is still working. You know they say they have baby-sitters of all kinds for all situations.'

'Oh, of course!' said Mrs Terrapin, looking delighted. 'Such nice reliable people. Perhaps you could ring them while I change.'

But Alpha, Oliver and Omega looked discontented. They did not enjoy having a baby-sitter. They thought they could take care of themselves. However they did not complain or kick the furniture, for they were good boys and liked to think of their mother having a happy evening out.

4. Mr Terrapin Rings Mother Goose

Mr Terrapin rang the Mother Goose Baby-Sitting Service at once.

A gracious voice answered, 'Mother Goose here! Who? Who is that? Ah, Mr Terrapin! And how are your little lads? Good! Good! And you want a baby-sitter? We have just the person for you ... Mr Orpheus Clinker, a

16

naval gentleman, but retired from the sea now. He will suit your boys, Mr Terrapin. He keeps order, and yet he's full of gentle fun. Yes, he'll be along in a quarter of an hour. Now – as to his supper ... do you have any rum in the house?'

'Rum?' cried Mr Terrapin. 'Rum? No – no, I don't drink it myself.'

'Ah, well, don't worry!' said Mother Goose. 'He'll no doubt bring his own. Now I must rush! The other phone's ringing. Good night, Mr Terrapin.'

5. The Baby-Sitter Arrives

A quarter of an hour later a curious hop-and-go-carry-one step sounded on the Terrapin path, and a curious clanging knock fell on the door. Mr Terrapin opened it and peered out.

'Mr Clinker?' he asked politely.

'What's left of him, matey,' growled a terrible voice. The baby-sitter shouldered Mr Terrapin roughly to one side and stumped into the kitchen. He wore a long green coat and had a polka-dot handkerchief tied around his head. He had one leg, wooden, and one arm, tin. He wore a patch over his left eye. It did seem that there was quite a lot of him missing, but what was left was more than enough. You certainly would not recognize him as a baby-sitter. Indeed it was plain to the most short-sighted landlubber (Mr Terrapin, for example) that Orpheus Clinker was a pirate. A large bottle of rum stuck out of his coat pocket. It was so big it weighed him down on one side.

Alpha, Oliver and Omega stared with open

mouths. 'At last,' they thought, 'a baby-sitter worthy of us – we deserve him, and he deserves us – what could be fairer than that?' They began to grin, and Orpheus Clinker himself began to grin, a salty fierce grin that ran and flashed all over his face like lightning over a battered sky.

'Well, you're three likely-looking lads, you are,' he declared. 'I thought the breed was extinct, I did. I didn't consider that there were any of us left among the Younger Generanium. I like the cut of your jib – your jibs, that is.'

The boys were pleased at having the cut of their jibs admired by the man of the sea.

6. Mr Terrapin Has a Moment of Doubt and Is Reassured

'Are you a – er – *practised* baby-sitter?' asked Mr Terrapin doubtfully. 'You don't *look* like a baby-sitter. You remind me of something else . . . I'll think of it in a moment . . . of something else . . .' his voice trailed off.

'Not to say *practised* exactly, matey,' admitted Orpheus Clinker. 'Not actually *practised*, as such. In fact, if you was to force me to utter honesty I'd have to confide that this is the first time the Mother Goose Computer has turned up my card.'

Mr Terrapin's fleeting doubts vanished, as he had a great respect for machines.

'So you were chosen by computer, were you?' he said. 'Very good, verr-y good.'

He hustled Mrs Terrapin out as quickly as he could, for they were already late for the important dinner, and he was afraid that they might miss the important soup.

7. *Orpheus Clinker Reveals His Secret Purposes*

'That's got rid of them,' said Orpheus Clinker, as the Terrapin parents went off up the drive. 'Mind you, I'm not saying a word against parents as such . . . my old mother was a saint in sheep's clothing . . . but there's no doubt that a lot of parents hanging around hamper a man in his activities.'

Alpha, Oliver and Omega nodded and grinned.

They knew just what he meant.

'Are you really a pirate, Mr Clinker?' asked Alpha courteously.

'A really real pirate?' demanded Oliver earnestly.

'A pirate?' squeaked little Omega, like an echo that needed oiling.

'Once I was, lads, once I was,' said Orpheus Clinker with a wistful sigh. 'I'm a retired man now. However, I'm not as retired as all that, and as I look around I can see that this house is just what I need for my secret purposes.'

'Secret purposes?' cried the Terrapin boys, hopeful and thrilled.

'Those who live . . .' said Orpheus Clinker, 'those who live, why they're the ones who will probably see. For I'm not the only pirate in this city, and this house is crying out for festivity and rumbustification. Come on out into the garden and we'll send a message.'

'A message?' cried Alpha and Oliver, beginning to fizz like fireworks.

'A message?' cried little Omega, beginning to bubble like lemonade.

'Yes, my hearties,' said Orpheus Clinker. 'The smell's right, the wind – why, it's brisk, isn't it? It's salt, isn't it?'

The boys sniffed the air and felt the wind. The wind was indeed brisk and salty, and the air smelled of excitement and mystery.

'Well,' said Orpheus Clinker, 'well then, we'll give a party . . . a pirate party, a Great Piratical Rumbustification – and all the pirates in town will come to drink and dine and dance.'

The boys were struck silent with amazement and delight.

Orpheus Clinker pulled his coat aside to reveal his pistol in his belt.

'I hid it from your parents, lads,' he said,

'for fear that it might cause despondency and
doubt. There's nothing like a pistol to bring out
despondency and doubt in a parent . . . now,
outside, and we'll let it off.'

24

'Who are we going to shoot?' asked Oliver.

'No one, silly,' replied Alpha. 'It's a distress flare, isn't it?'

'No, lad, no. It's a festive flare,' explained Orpheus Clinker. 'A pirate-party flare! A signal for conviviality and rumbustification. One glimpse of this and all the pirates in the metropolis will be wiping their boots on your doormat (or failing to wipe them, as the case may be with them as is not brought up proper).'

Out on the lawn, Orpheus stood with the boys around him. He pointed his pistol at the sky and pulled the trigger. There was a pop like a cork coming out of a bottle of very powerful ginger beer. The sky above the Terrapin House was filled with dazzling green, gold, blue and scarlet. The boys shouted and pranced for wonder and pleasure at the sight.

'The flares, d'ye see, catch the attention of every pirate in the city,' explained Orpheus Clinker. 'The smoke spells out the message. It's educated smoke, that it is. And so the word gets around.'

Like threads of silver the smoke trails twisted themselves into words, spelling out a message across the stars.

'Pirate Party,' read Alpha, 'Pirate Party.'

'But how will they know where to come?' asked Oliver.

'They're sailors, aren't they?' asked Orpheus Clinker. 'There'll be pirates all over town, a-reading of those lovely words, and a-getting of

their bearings . . . But we mustn't waste our time.
I've brought steak and onions with me. We
must begin the pirate stew. Do you think your
lady mother would mind if I borrowed her
apron?'

8. Mr Terrapin Feels Jealous

Across town in a new and startling dine-and-dance establishment Mr Terrapin supped his first mouthful of the important soup. He sighed. The soup wasn't worth all the hurry to get to it. There was something missing. He looked around for the salt but could see none within his reach.

Just then something caught his eye through the big window. Mr Terrapin looked again. He was amazed to see the sky lit up with stars – green and gold, blue and scarlet – and the words 'PIRATE PARTY', scribbled in silver smoke.

'Someone is having a good party in that direction,' he said enviously. Mrs Terrapin looked too.

'Why,' she said, 'it looks as if it's over our part of town.'

'Nonsense!' said Mr Terrapin, quite crossly. 'No one ever gives a party like that in our part of town.'

'A party like what?' asked Mrs Terrapin, blinking. (Sometimes she found it hard to follow Mr Terrapin.)

'Like that!' said Mr Terrapin. 'I'll bet there is plenty of salt in their soup ... Why, that doesn't look like a mere party to me. That looks more like a rumbustification, that does.'

He gave another jealous glance out of the window.

Mr Terrapin would have been amazed to find out just how much salt there was at the rumbustification in question.

The rumbustification wasn't a rumbustification yet, however. Like ragged butterflies, like autumn leaves blown out of hiding, pirates came from all parts of the city to the Terrapin House.

Some came in such a hurry they did not have time to put on their pirate clothes. They just came as ordinary grey-haired distinguished

lawyers and business men. But most of them put on some of their pirate raggle-taggle: their cheerful silk 'kerchiefs, their gold earrings and their cutlasses. Parrots sat on their shoulders. They played mouth-organs and old brown fiddles as they came. They turned the footpaths of the city into a pirate chain-dance, they turned the streets into a pirate parade.

Suddenly the city seemed to twist and spin and sing like a big humming top. The pirates were spinning it, as they walked and ran and

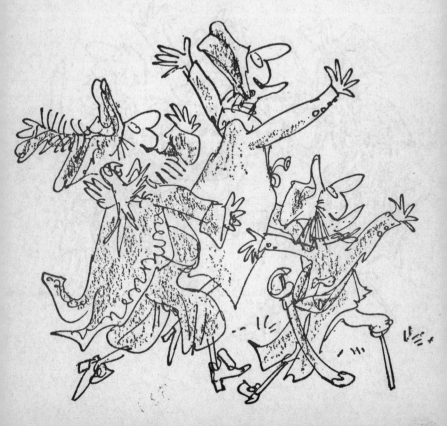

drove back to the Terrapin House. Already the air was rich with the smell of the beginning of pirate stew.

Standing on the steps of Terrapin House as if it were his very own, Orpheus Clinker looked like a pirate, a cook and a king all rolled into one magnificent figure.

As for Alpha, Oliver and Omega, they had tried to dress as pirate cabin boys. They had silk scarves belonging to Mrs Terrapin tied around their heads. They looked like sparrows with the crests of peacocks and birds of paradise.

There was no need for any introduction. With shouts of joy they welcomed the pirates in.

The great pirate party had begun.

10. Terrible Crabmeat

One particular pirate was late, and that was the oldest, wickedest pirate of all. His name was Terrible Crabmeat. He was getting dressed to go to another party altogether when he saw the message in the sky. He was already late for that party too, but then he did not care about manners. When he saw there was a chance of piratical festivity, he changed his mind entirely. He called for his pirate clothes, his wheel-chair and his cutlass. His servant brought him his clothes and cutlass and helped him put them on. Then he assisted him into his wheel-chair (for Terrible Crabmeat was a hundred and five, and rather crippled with age and various

kinds of wickedness). This wheelchair was a very expensive one with a motor and a sharp impatient horn. On the back of it was a skull and crossbones, painted by a famous artist.

'Off again!' muttered Terrible Crabmeat with quiet relish.

'Yes, indeed, Sir John,' said his devoted servant (for Terrible Crabmeat went under the name of 'Sir John' to make his wealth seem respectable). 'I hope you have an enjoyable evening.'

'I shall,' said Terrible Crabmeat cackling with terrible glee, 'I shall. It's been a long time since there was any sort of rumbustification. Ha! I can still make them jump. Yes, they'll still jump when I say jump, or I'll know the reason why.'

So saying he pressed the starter, the wheel-chair shot forwards, and off he went – a strange and fearsome figure, heading for the Terrapin house, heading for the Great Piratical Rumbustification which was already under way.

11. *In the Meantime Mr Terrapin Feels Disgruntled*

Mr Terrapin was feeling disgruntled. He got crosser and crosser as the important dinner carried on to its close. Nothing had enough salt in it. The rich man he had wanted to meet, and to observe closely, had not turned up. Mr Terrapin felt he had been tricked, but he was not sure who had tricked him. It was this that made him disgruntled. He longed for the dinner to be over, but it took a long time. Then there were speeches. They were longer. As soon as he could, Mr Terrapin took Mrs Terrapin out to their car and began to drive her home.

'I don't think parties are what they were,' he said as he drove. 'I remember parties that went off with a bang and seemed to fill the air with rainbows and parrot feathers.'

'My dear,' said Mrs Terrapin gently, 'you've grown older since those days.'

'And then Sir John did not turn up,' Mr Terrapin grumbled.

'My dear, he's a hundred and five,' said Mrs Terrapin. 'He's probably gone to bed with a hot water bottle and a glass of warm milk. Or perhaps he was stopped by the police. I'm told he goes very fast in that wheelchair of his.'

'Silly old fool!' snapped Mr Terrapin. He leaned out of the window of the car. 'That's funny! Why is the sky lit up in our part of the city? There's something going on, I tell you.' A moment later he cried to Mrs Terrapin, 'It's at our house! . . . Yes, Millie, it's at our house. Someone has lighted a bonfire on the terrace. Good heavens! The place is full of pirates! Well, that's the last time we ever deal with the Mother Goose Baby-Sitting Service.'

'Now, Henry, don't be hasty,' said Mrs Terrapin, surveying the milling throng of pirates with amazement. 'There may be a perfectly reasonable explanation to all this.'

'Pigs might fly!' exclaimed Mr Terrapin. But by now he was as wild and furious as the most wild and furious pirate. For he could see that the great pirate party was nearly at its height. Music flowed like rum, and rum flowed

like music. Every house in the street was empty. In a great whirlpool of noise and brightness, the pirate party had sucked in all the neighbours and passers-by. Neighbours and passers-by had changed hats with the pirates. You could not tell one from the other, unless you looked closely, and not always then. The noise was tremendous.

But Mr Terrapin was equal to the occasion.

He drove right across the lawn on to the terrace, scattering pirates right and left. Then he leaped from the car shouting sternly, 'What is the meaning of this?'

There was a sudden deep silence. No one could think for a moment of any meaning that seemed good enough. Not even a parrot screamed. Alpha, Oliver and Omega who had been dancing a moment ago stopped still, stricken with dismay. They had hoped their father would understand.

'You said we could do something adventurous when we got into a bigger house...' Alpha was beginning. But suddenly the crowd parted and out came Terrible Crabmeat, more terrible than ever in his wheelchair.

'The meaning of it?' he croaked. 'It doesn't have to mean anything. This is a stolen party – a peppery, parroty party, a pirate party. In fact, it's more than a party ... it's a Great Piratical Rumbustification, and we've chosen you to be our host, Terrapin.'

Mr Terrapin's mouth had opened with surprise. 'Sir John . . .' he began, 'why, Sir John! I didn't realize . . . I didn't recognize you! If you are here, the party must be more respectable than it seemed at first.'

'If you think that,' said Sir-John-Terrible-Crabmeat, 'then you are a noodle. But in the meantime, relax and enjoy yourself. Come and talk to me for a moment. And call me Crabmeat! It's my real name, you know.'

Everyone could see Mr Terrapin suddenly grow easy in his mind. And then the party began again. It was like fireworks, whizzing and buzzing and going off *bang*, filling the air with rainbows and parrot feathers.

12. *Now Mr Terrapin Enjoys the Party*

At last a party Mr Terrapin could enjoy! Suddenly he became more of a pirate than anyone. He sang and played the tambourine. He did a wicked pirate hornpipe. When the pirate stew was served, he ate three bowlsful. Alpha, Oliver and Omega were amazed and delighted at his activities. They pointed him out and boasted to people that he was their father. For his part Mr Terrapin was delighted to hear his three boys so praised and admired.

'They're the right stuff, they are,' said Terrible Crabmeat warmly. 'They'll get on in the world, they will. I only wish I had such spirits when I was a lad.'

When the pirate stew was all eaten, Orpheus Clinker himself washed the stew pot and took it to Terrible Crabmeat. 'Bang on it, man,' cried Terrible Crabmeat in a voice half-croak half-cackle. Orpheus banged on the pot with his hook, causing it to ring like a bell.

'Show your gratitude, swabs!' he bellowed. 'He that calls for the tune, why he's the one

that pays the piper, isn't he, now?' He pointed to the empty stew pot he was holding.

One by one the pirates filed past and soon the yard was echoing to the chink and jingle of treasure. Doubloons and pieces of eight fell into the empty pot. Jewels and pearls sparkled and shone among them.

'Pirate bells, pirate bells!' said Orpheus

Clinker out of the corner of his mouth to Alpha, Oliver and Omega. 'Ring out lovely, don't they?'

'It makes it seem true – pirates-and-treasure,' said little Omega.

'It's been a beautiful rumbustification. Will it happen again?' asked Oliver.

'Will it happen again?' cried Orpheus Clinker. 'Well, I'll tell you this. I've never met three more likely lads than yourselves, as I may have mentioned, and once a pirate, always a pirate. And Great Piratical Rumbustifications always come again!'

'It's the best rumbustification we've ever had,' said another pirate, and Terrible Crabmeat agreed.

The stew pot was filled to the brim. Terrible Crabmeat pointed to it and said to Mr Terrapin: 'There you are, Terrapin, there's cheer for you. It is our custom to make our host an honorary pirate and equip him with treasure. That's your share. Guard it well.'

Mr Terrapin looked at the treasure with delight. He would be able to pay for his house and still have plenty left over. The troubles that had beset him the last few weeks vanished like the merest mist – no more turning green and going all limp. He felt contentment pour into his heart like creamy milk into a porridge bowl.

Mr Terrapin was restless no more.

The pirates had stopped feeling restless, too.

Full of piratical comradeship, and piratical stew, they drifted homeward in the early spring morning, like ragged butterflies, like tattered bright birds. Even the parrots were too tired to screech and flutter.

By the time the sun rose there wasn't a pirate in sight. They were all asleep. They weren't even dreaming.

Mingled with the rumble of cars and buses, was the rumble of pirate snores. It could be heard all over the city. (But you had to listen very closely.)

As for Alpha, Oliver and Omega – they were good for a long time afterwards.

13. *How It Ended!*

Everything had ended happily – almost. Almost, because spring is followed by summer, and summer by autumn and winter. Towards the end of winter, with the beginning of a new spring a curious feeling comes into the city. Most people don't understand it.

'There's a funny feeling in the air,' they say.

But Alpha, Oliver and Omega know what it is, and welcome it with joy.

The pirates are beginning to be restless again.

THE LIBRARIAN
AND
THE ROBBERS

One day Serena Laburnum, the beautiful librarian, was carried off by wicked robbers. She had just gone for a walk in the woods at the edge of the town, when the robbers came charging at her and carried her off.

'Why are you kidnapping me?' she asked coldly. 'I have no wealthy friends or relatives. Indeed I am an orphan with no real home but the library.'

'That's just it,' said the Robber Chief. 'The City Council will pay richly to have you restored. After all, everyone knows that the library does not work properly without you.'

This was especially true because Miss Laburnum had the library keys.

'I think I ought to warn you,' she said, 'that I spent the weekend with a friend of mine who has four little boys. Everyone in the house had the dread disease of Raging Measles.'

'That's all right!' said the Robber Chief, sneering a bit. 'I've had them.'

'But I haven't!' said the robber at his elbow, and the other robbers looked at Miss Laburnum uneasily. None of them had had the dread disease of Raging Measles.

As soon as the robbers' ransom note was received by the City Council, there was a lot of discussion. Everyone was anxious that things should be done in the right way.

'What is it when our librarian is kidnapped?' asked a councillor. 'Is it staff expenditure or does it come out of the cultural fund?'

'The Cultural Committee meets in a fortnight,' said the Mayor. 'I propose we let them make a decision on this.'

But long before that, all the robbers (except the Robber Chief) had Raging Measles.

First of all they became very irritable and had red sniffy noses.

'I *think* a hot bath brings out the rash,' said Miss Laburnum doubtfully. 'Oh, if only I were in my library I would be able to look up measles in my *Dictionary of Efficient and Efficacious Home Nursing.*'

The Robber Chief looked gloomily at his gang.

'Are you sure it's measles?' he said. 'That's a

very undignified complaint for a robber to suffer from. There are few people who are improved by spots, but for robbers they are disastrous. Would you take a spotty robber seriously?'

'It is no part of a librarian's duty to take any robber seriously, spotty or otherwise,' said Miss Laburnum haughtily. 'And, anyhow, there must be no robbing until they have got over the Raging Measles. They are in quarantine. After all you don't want to be blamed for spreading measles everywhere, do you?'

The Robber Chief groaned.

'If you will allow me,' said Miss Laburnum, 'I will go back to my library and borrow *The Dictionary of Efficient and Efficacious Home Nursing*. With the help of that invaluable book I shall try to alleviate the sufferings of your fellows. Of course I shall only be able to take it out for a week. It is a special reference book, you see.'

The groaning of his fellows suffering from Raging Measles was more than the Robber Chief could stand.

'All right,' he said. 'You can go and get that book, and we'll call off the kidnapping for the present. Just a temporary measure.'

In a short time Miss Laburnum was back with several books.

'A hot bath to bring out the rash!' she announced reading clearly and carefully. 'Then

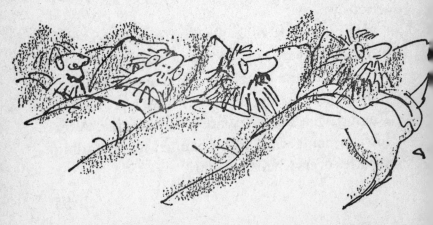

you must have the cave darkened, and you mustn't read or play cards. You have to be careful of your eyes when you have measles.'

The robbers found it very dull, lying in a darkened cave. Miss Laburnum took their temperatures and asked them if their ears hurt.

'It's very important that you keep warm,' she told them, pulling blankets up to their robberish beards, and tucking them in so tightly that they could not toss or turn. 'But to make the time go quickly I will read to you. Now, what have you read already?'

These robbers had not read a thing. They were almost illiterate. 'Very well,' said Miss Laburnum, 'we shall start with Peter Rabbit and work our way up from there.'

Never in all their lives had those robbers been read to. In spite of the fever induced by Raging Measles they listened intently and asked for more. The Robber Chief listened too, though Miss Laburnum had given him the task of making nourishing broth for the invalids.

'Tell us more about that Br'er Rabbit!' was the fretful cry of the infectious villains. 'Read to us about Alice in Wonderland.'

Robin Hood made them uneasy. He was a robber, as they were, but full of noble thoughts such as giving to the poor. These robbers had not planned on giving to the poor, but only on keeping for themselves.

After a few days the spots began to disappear, and the robbers began to get hungry. Miss Laburnum dipped into her *Dictionary of Efficient and Efficacious Home Nursing*, and found some tempting recipes for the convalescent. She wrote them out for the Robber Chief. Having given up the idea of kidnapping Miss Laburnum, the Robber Chief now had the idea of kidnapping the book, but Miss Laburnum wouldn't let him have it.

'It is used by a lot of people who belong to the library,' she said. 'But, of course, if you want to check up on anything later you may always come to the library and consult it.'

Shortly after this the robbers were quite recovered and Miss Laburnum, with her keys, went back to town. It seemed that robbers were a thing of the past. *The Dictionary of Efficient and Efficacious Home Nursing* was restored to the library shelves. The library was open once more to the hordes who had been starved for literature during the days of Miss Laburnum's kidnapping.

Yet, about three weeks after all these dramatic events, there was more robber trouble!

Into the library, in broad daylight, burst none other than the Robber Chief.

'Save me!' he cried. 'A policeman is after me.'

Miss Laburnum gave him a cool look.

'You had better give me your full name,' she said. 'Quickly!'

The Robber Chief sprang back, an expression of horror showing through his black tangled beard.

'No, no!' he cried, 'anything but that!'

'Quickly,' repeated Miss Laburnum, 'or I won't have time to help you.'

The Robber Chief leaned across the desk and whispered his name to her ... 'Salvation Loveday.'

Miss Laburnum could not help smiling a little bit. It certainly went very strangely with those wiry whiskers.

'They used to call me Sally at school,' cried the unhappy robber. 'It's that name that has driven me to a life of crime. But hide me, dear Miss Laburnum, or I shall be caught.'

Miss Laburnum stamped him with a number, as if he was a library book, and put him into a bookshelf with a lot of books whose authors had surnames beginning with 'L'. He was in strict alphabetical order. Alphabetical order is a habit with librarians.

The policeman who had been chasing the Robber Chief burst into the library. He was a good runner, but he had fallen over a little boy on a tricycle, and this had slowed him down.

'Miss Laburnum,' said the policeman, 'I have just had occasion to pursue a notable Robber Chief into your library. I can see him there in the bookshelves among the L's. May I take him out please?'

'Certainly!' said Miss Laburnum pleasantly.

'Do you have your library membership card?'

The policeman's face fell.

'Oh dear,' he said. 'No . . . I'm afraid it's at home marking the place in my *Policeman's Robber-Catching Compendium.*'

Miss Laburnum gave a polite smile.

'I'm afraid you can't withdraw anything without your membership card,' she said. 'That Robber Chief is Library Property.'

The policeman nodded slowly. He knew it was true: you weren't allowed to take anything out of the library without your library card. This was a strict library rule. 'I'll just tear home and get it,' he said. 'I don't live very far away.'

'Do that,' said Miss Laburnum pleasantly. The policeman's strong police boots rang out as he hurried from the library.

Miss Laburnum went to the 'L' shelf and took down the Robber Chief. 'Now, what are you doing *here*?' she said severely. However, the Robber Chief was not fooled – she was really very pleased to see him.

'Well,' he replied, 'the fact is, Miss Laburnum, my men are restless. Ever since you read them those stories, they've been discontented in the evening. We used to sit around our campfire singing rumbustical songs and indulging in rough humour, but they've lost their taste for it. They're wanting more *Br'er Rabbit*, more *Treasure Island*, and more stories of kings and clowns. Today I was coming to join the library and take some books out for them. What shall I do? I daren't go back without books, and yet that policeman may return. And won't he be very angry with you when he finds I'm gone?'

'That will be taken care of,' said Miss Laburnum, smiling to herself. 'What is your number? Ah, yes. Well, when the policeman returns, I will tell him someone else has taken you out, and it will be true, for you are now issued to me.'

The Robber Chief gave Miss Laburnum a very speaking look.

'And now,' said Miss Laburnum cheerfully, 'you must join the library yourself and take out some books for your poor robbers.'

'If I am a member of the library myself, perhaps I could take you out,' said the Robber Chief with robberish boldness. Miss Laburnum quickly changed the subject, but she blushed as she did so.

She sent the Robber Chief off with some splendid story books.

He had only just gone when the policeman came back.

'Now,' said the policeman, producing his membership card, 'I'd like to take out that Robber Chief, if I may.'

He looked so expectant it seemed a pity to disappoint him. Miss Laburnum glanced towards the L's.

'Oh,' she said, 'I'm afraid he has already been taken out by someone else. You should have reserved him.'

The policeman stared at the shelf very hard. Then he stared at Miss Laburnum.

'May I put my name down for him?' he asked after a moment.

'Certainly,' said Miss Laburnum, 'though I ought to warn you that you may have a long wait ahead of you. There could be a long waiting list.'

After this the Robber Chief came sneaking into town regularly to change books. It was dangerous, but he thought it was worth it.

As the robbers read more and more, their culture and philosophy deepened, until they were the most cultural and philosophic band of robbers one could wish to encounter. As for Miss Laburnum, there is no doubt that she was aiding and abetting robbers; not very good behaviour in a librarian, but she had her reasons.

Then came the day of the terrible earthquake. Chimneys fell down all over town. Every building creaked and rattled. Out in the forest the robbers felt it and stood aghast as trees swayed and pinecones came tumbling around them like hailstones. At last the ground was still again. The Robber Chief went pale.

'The library!' he called. 'What will have happened to Miss Laburnum and the books?'

Every other robber turned pale too. You never saw such a lot of pale-faced robbers at one and the same time.

'Quickly!' they shouted. 'To the rescue! Rescue! Rescue Miss Laburnum. Save the books.'

Shouting such words as these they all ran down the road out of the forest and into town.

The policeman saw them, but when he heard their heroic cry he decided to help them first and arrest them afterwards.

'Save Miss Laburnum!' he shouted. 'Rescue the books.'

What a terrible scene in the library! Pictures had fallen from the walls and the flowers were upset. Boxes of stamps were overturned and mixed up all over the floor. Books had fallen from their shelves like autumn leaves from their

trees, and lay all over the floor in helpless confusion.

There was no sign of Miss Laburnum that anyone could see.

Actually Miss Laburnum had been shelving books in the old store – the shelves where they put all the battered old books – when the earthquake came. Ancient, musty encyclopaedias showered down upon her. When the earthquake was over she was still alive, but so covered in books that she could not move.

'Pulverized by literature,' thought Miss Laburnum. 'The ideal way for a librarian to die.'

She did not feel very pleased about it, but there was nothing she could do to save herself. Then she heard a heroic cry!

'Serena, Serena Laburnum!' a voice was shouting. Someone was pulling books off her. It was the Robber Chief.

'Salvation is a very good name for you,' said Miss Laburnum faintly.

Tenderly he lifted her to her feet and dusted her down.

'I came as soon as I could,' he said. 'Oh, Miss Laburnum, this may not be the best time to ask you, but as I am giving up a life of crime and becoming respectable, will you marry me? You need someone to lift the books off you, and generally rescue you from time to time. It would make things so much simpler if you would marry me.'

'Of course I will,' said Miss Laburnum simply. 'After all, I did take you out with my library membership card; I must have secretly admired you for a long time.'

Out in the main room of the library there was great activity. Robbers and councillors, working together like brothers, were sorting the mixed-up stamps, filing the spilled cards, reshelving the fallen books. The policeman was hanging up some of the pictures. They all cheered when the Robber Chief appeared with Miss Laburnum, bruised but still beautiful.

'Ahem,' said the Robber Chief. 'I am the happiest man alive. Miss Laburnum has promised to marry me.'

A great cheer went up from everyone.

'On one condition,' said Miss Laburnum. 'That all you robbers give up being robbers and become librarians instead. You weren't very good at being robbers, but I think as librarians you might be excellent. I have come to feel very proud of you all.'

The robbers were struck to breathless silence. Never when they were mere inefficient robbers in the forest had they dreamed of such praise. Greatly moved by these sentiments they then and there swore that they would cease to be villains and become librarians instead.

It was all very exciting. Even the policeman wept with joy.

So, ever after, that particular library was remarkably well run. With all the extra librarians they suddenly had, the council was able to open a children's library with story readings and adventure plays every day. The robber librarians had become very good at such things practising around their campfires in the forest.

Miss Laburnum, or Mrs Loveday as she soon became, sometimes suspected that the children's library in their town was – well – a little wilder, a little more humorous, than many other fine libraries she had seen, but she did not care. She did not mind that the robber librarians all wore wiry black whiskers still, nor that they took down all the notices saying 'Silence' and 'No talking in the library'.

Perhaps she herself was more of a robber at heart than anyone ever suspected . . .

except, of course, Robber-Chief-and-First-Library-Assistant Salvation Loveday, and he did not tell anyone.

Some other Young Puffins

ZOZU THE ROBOT
Diana Carter

Rufus and Sarah found the Thing in the garden. It looked like a ball, but it buzzed, it changed colour, and it *talked*. Zozu turns out to be a tiny metal creature, not a bit like the huge, scary visitors from space that Rufus and Sarah had always imagined.

RAT SATURDAY
Margaret Nash

A sensitive and appealing story showing how a boy who feels inferior comes to make friends with his neighbours and schoolmates. An old man, reputed to be a tramp, invites him to visit his pet rats and gradually their friendship grows, so that together they manage to solve each other's problems.

MR BERRY'S ICE-CREAM PARLOUR
Jennifer Zabel

Carl is thrilled when Mr Berry, the new lodger, comes to stay. But when Mr Berry announces his plan to open an ice-cream parlour, Carl can hardly believe it. And this is just the start of the excitement in store when Mr Berry walks through the door!

THE DEAD LETTER BOX
Jan Mark

Louie got the idea from an old film which showed how spies left their letters in a secret place – a dead letter box. It was just the kind of thing that she and Glenda needed to help them keep in touch. And she knew the perfect place for it!

CHANGING OF THE GUARD and WALLPAPER HOLIDAY
H. E. Todd

Two delightful stories about the adventures of Timothy Trumper and his family. Ideal for reading aloud.

KATY AND THE NURGLA
Harry Secombe

Katy had the whole beach to herself, until an old tired monster swam up to the very rocks where she was sitting reading. Harry Secombe's first book for children has all the best ingredients in the right proportions: a monster, a space-ship, adventure, humour and more than a touch of happy sadness.

PROFESSOR BRANESTAWM'S POCKET MOTOR CAR
Norman Hunter

Two Branestawm stories especially written for younger readers: the Professor's amazing genius for invention produces an inflatable car to solve parking problems, and an extremely clever letter-writing machine.

THE WORST WITCH
THE WORST WITCH STRIKES AGAIN
A BAD SPELL FOR THE WORST WITCH
Jill Murphy

Mildred Hubble is the most disastrous dunce of all at Miss Cackle's Academy for witches. But even Mildred has the occasional good spell! Jolly broomsticks and brimstone in these very different school stories.

WORZEL GUMMIDGE AT THE FAIR
Keith Waterhouse and Willis Hall

Here he is again – the scatty Worzel Gummidge – neglecting his crow-scaring and trying to win back Aunt Sally from a fairground Strong Man. But the path of true love isn't easy for Worzel – especially when he meets another pretty scarecrow . . .

UPSIDE DOWN STORIES
Donald Bisset

Brilliant nonsense tales to delight children, telling about such oddities as an inexperienced apple tree which grows squirrels instead of apples!

DORRIE AND THE BIRTHDAY EGGS
Patricia Coombs

When the eggs for the Big Witch's birthday cake get broken by mistake, Dorrie sets off to buy some more from the Egg Witch. But her errand takes her through the forest, and lurking there is Thinnever Vetch, all ready to make mischief . . .

ALLOTMENT LANE SCHOOL AGAIN
Margaret Joy

It's always fun in Miss Mee's class and now the holidays are over and everyone is glad to be back at Allotment Lane School again. Fourteen lively stories about Class 1 and their friends.

HANK PRANK AND HOT HENRIETTA
Jules Older

Hank and his hot-tempered sister, Henrietta, are always getting themselves into touble but the doings of this terrible pair make for an entertaining series of adventures.